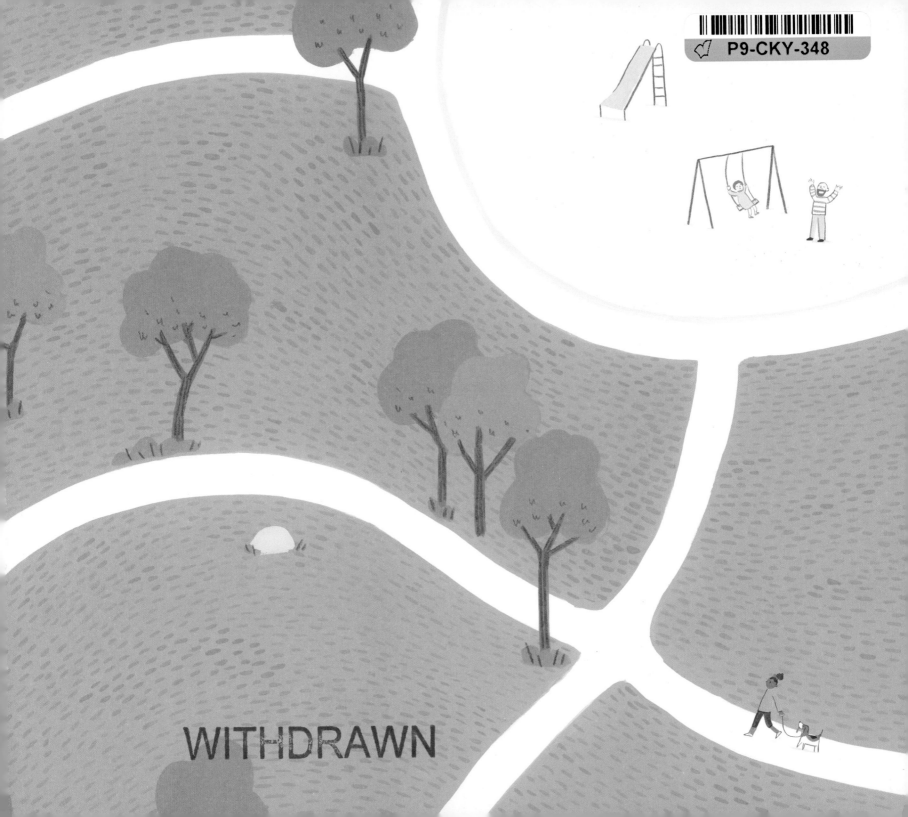

LOST THINGS

FOR ALBERT. I WOULD BE LOST WITHOUT YOU.

Published in Canada and the U.S. by Kids Can Press Ltd.
25 Dockside Drive, Toronto, ON M5A 0B5

Kids Can Press is a Corus Entertainment Inc. company

www.kidscanpress.com

The artwork in this book was rendered traditionally using acrylic gouache and drawing pencil.
The text is set in Apercu.

Edited by Debbie Rogosin
Designed by Marie Bartholomew

Printed and bound in Buji, Shenzhen, China, in 3/2021 by WKT Company

CM 21 0 9 8 7 6 5 4 3 2 1

LIBRARY AND ARCHIVES CANADA CATALOGUING IN PUBLICATION

Title: Lost things / [written and illustrated by] Carey Sookocheff
Names: Sookocheff, Carey, 1972– author, illustrator.
Identifiers: Canadiana 20200364529 | ISBN 9781525305443 (hardcover)
Classification: LCC PS8637.O56 L67 2021 | DDC jC813/.6 — dc23

Kids Can Press gratefully acknowledges that the land on which our office is located is the traditional territory of many nations, including the Mississaugas of the Credit, the Anishnabeg, the Chippewa, the Haudenosaunee and the Wendat peoples, and is now home to many diverse First Nations, Inuit and Métis peoples.

We thank the Government of Ontario, through Ontario Creates; the Ontario Arts Council; the Canada Council for the Arts; and the Government of Canada for supporting our publishing activity.

LOST
THINGS

CAREY SOOKOCHEFF

KIDS CAN PRESS

Sometimes things are lost.

Once in a while,

lost things

find a new home.

Sometimes,

lost things

have to wait to be found.

Other times,

they aren't missed at all.

But can become

someone else's treasure.

And from time to time,

lost things are found

by the people who need them the most.

Just when they need them.